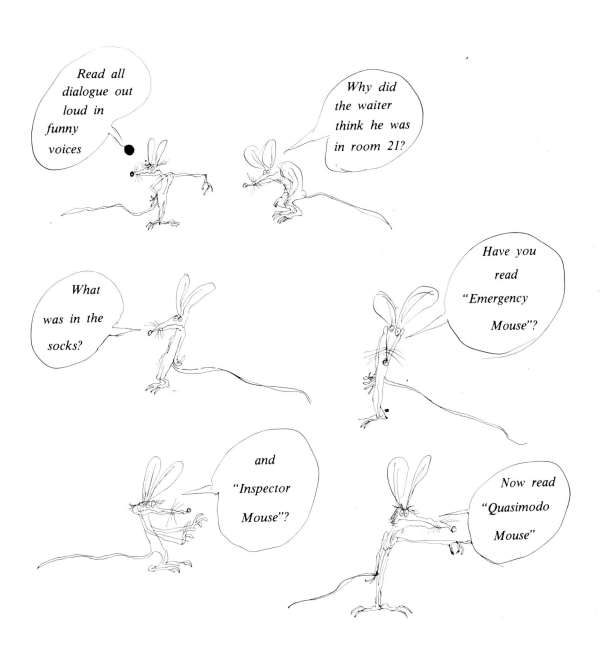

Andersen Press · London
Hutchinson of Australia

Quasimodo MOUSE

Bernard STONE and Ralph STEADman

Quasimodo Mouse flopped heavily
against the cathedral parapet and
groaned. "Phew! Enough is
enough. Ringing bells in this hot
weather is no fun. All my friends
are living it up by the sea. It's time
I got out of here."
So he left Paris, his beloved city of
soot and memories. Once outside
the city, he took a last lingering
look over the rooftops towards the
great cathedral that towered in the
distance. Then without another
backward glance, he set his red
nose southwards and limped on.

As the sun rose higher in the sky, the heat made him tired and he stopped to rest. "What I need right now is a lift," he thought as he mopped his brow.

At that precise moment, an eager little figure astride a tandem whizzed past him along the road. There was no one on the back seat. "Stop!" yelled Quasimodo, flagging down the driver whom he recognised as none other than his old friend Toothy. "This is what friends are for," he said, making himself comfortable on the back seat.

They zoomed off in a cloud of country dust, passing through one village after another. Quasimodo was enchanted by the changing landscape. Toothy's eyes were on the road. It was all just a blur to him.

"How much further have we got to go? I'm getting hungry," said Quasimodo after a while. "Can we stop?"

"Stop! What for?" shouted Toothy. "We've only just started." His voice trailed off in the wind.

"I'm still hungry,"
Quasimodo said a few
miles further on.
"And there are apples over
there."
"Apples?" Toothy sounded
interested. "Where? I love
apples."
"There," replied
Quasimodo pointing.
"That's different," Toothy
shouted as they screeched
to a halt.
"I'll always stop for
apples."
And so they did.

After apples they both felt good. Good enough to leave the road behind them and to zoom off across the countryside. It was very bumpy. After what seemed like ages Quasimodo said, "Don't you think we should stop for the night? We have no lights."

"Stop again?" shouted Toothy. "We'll never get there."

"What's the hurry?" replied Quasimodo. "Don't you like eating?"

"Of course," said Toothy. "Why didn't you say eating if that's what you meant?" So they stopped.

They reached a small old inn, where the walls seemed to have built themselves.
The innkeeper greeted them. "A room for two? Certainly, sirs. And with a
shower and toilet?"
"This is wonderful," mused Toothy as he sipped a glass of rich, dark
blackcurrant wine.

Bedtime was bliss.
"There's nothing like it," sighed
Quasimodo. As soon as his huge
head touched the pillow, his mind
swam away to dreamland, while he
lay snug and warm under the
bedclothes.

Toothy was not so lucky. He
tossed and turned and could not
sleep.

"Oh, good Lord," he groaned. "I've
got to get to sleep or I'll never be
any good tomorrow." But, no
matter how hard he tried, he could
not get his eyes to stay closed.

"Oooooooooooooooh!" went an
awful moan.

Toothy shot up in bed. "What
the – W-w-w-what do you want?"
he stammered, almost beside
himself with fear.

Before him stood a white ghost
trembling in the moonlight.

"Give me your socks," wailed the
ghost.

"I don't wear socks," whispered
Toothy nervously.

"No socks?"

"No socks," repeated Toothy.

"But isn't this Room 21?" wailed
the ghost.

"Room 22, I think," said Toothy,
shaking all over. "Wake up,
Quasimodo! There's a mad ghost
in the room. He's after our socks."

Quasimodo awoke and peeped over the bedclothes. "Socks?" he mumbled sleepily. "We don't wear socks."
Nevertheless, when he saw the ghost, he pulled the most horrible face you ever saw, and he was, after all, the champion face-puller in all of France.
"Aaargh," he yelled.
"Aaaaaargh!" screamed the ghost, and leapt out of his skin, which was only an old sheet anyway.
"It's only Waiter Mouse," sighed Toothy with relief as Waiter Mouse fled. "You scared me too though, but thank you."
"Goodnight, Toothy," said Quasimodo. "Now go to sleep. You've got a lot of pedalling to do tomorrow."

Next day they were off at the crack of dawn.

"How beautiful everything is," thought Quasimodo as he looked around him. "Aren't the colours lovely, Toothy?"

"Lovely," replied Toothy watching the road carefully. "Keep pedalling."

"Look out!" shouted Quasimodo. "That looks like hay."

Too late. It was hay. Legs, wheels, arms and noses went everywhere. And worse still, the hay was being painted by Pissarro Mouse, the local artist.

"Oh dear," wailed Pissarro Mouse. "Now I'll have to start again. I told you not to move, Miss Pinktwist – and keep that child still."

There was hay everywhere. Quasimodo and Toothy apologised to Pissarro Mouse who was steaming with anger, wiping his brushes on his ears.

Then they went on their way.

"The sea can't be far now," said Toothy.

Over another hill,

across a pretty bridge,

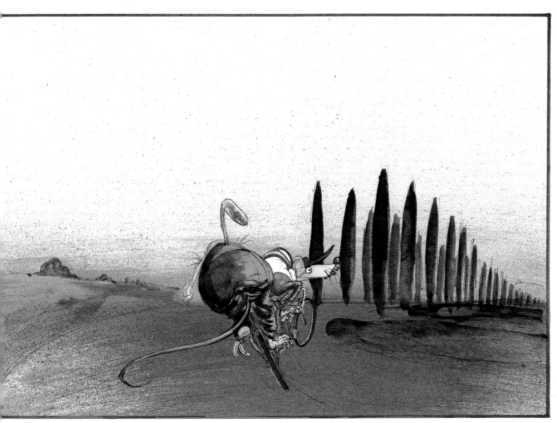

around a sharp bend,

and the home run. They freewheeled down into the harbour of Cassis.

Quasimodo jumped off the bicycle
and rolled over and over in the
sand.

"This is the life," he said happily.

"I'm off to find our friends," called
Toothy. "See you later, Quasi."

Quasimodo sat up and looked
around him. The sun shone down.
He was tired but he felt good. It
had been a good idea to come.
He started to make a sandcastle.
Gradually it became more and
more like the great cathedral he
had left behind him.

"The children seem to like it too,"
he sighed to himself as he worked.

Suddenly Quasimodo heard a terrible scream.
"Someone must be in trouble," he thought, as he looked out to sea.

There he saw a pair of arms waving wildly in the water. He flung his gigantic hump to the ground and stood glistening in the sunlight. "Hold on. I'll save you," he shouted and dived into the blue waters like a dolphin.

Gathering up the poor creature in his arms he swam to safety.

"Daisy," he exclaimed in surprise as he put her down gently. She was the beggar girl whom he had often seen listening to the cathedral bells in Paris. "What are you doing here?"

"I came south to get a job," she replied. "But all I've been able to do is to earn a little cheese by singing with the local band, Les Roquefours."

"My favourite band," whooped Quasimodo. "And there they are," he said, pointing to his friends who had come down to the beach to greet him. "Help me on with my hump, Daisy," he said. "We're going out on the town tonight."

Les Roquefours played wild music
as Quasimodo and Daisy danced
the night away.

"Dig that sentence," crooned Joe
Mozzarella, the band's leader, who
had just come out of jail.

"With a record like his, the music
should be good," muttered
Inspector Mouse.

"It's full of bars, man," agreed
Hunter Hipmouse.

"Come back to Paris with me,"
whispered Quasimodo to his
swooning partner. "We can dance
to our own tune there."

As a wedding present Toothy gave
them the tandem bicycle and off
they went.

Along the quay, they stopped to
watch the sun rise on another
beautiful day.

"It's only eight hundred and forty
kilometres to Paris," sighed Daisy.

"Yes, my love. But we'll take it
slowly," replied Quasimodo.

"We'll go back the pretty way. I'll
keep my eyes on the road and
steer. You can look at the
landscape and pedal."

PARIS 840 Kms
Total Direction